1.

When I wake up, I have blood on my teeth and flesh in my mouth and my face is hot, and sticky. Hair from my matted fringe is glued across my forehead. My limbs ache. I'm not wearing anything except someone else's insides. I can feel slippery links of intestines sliding across my belly. Not mine. All the parts of me that matter are safe beneath my skin.

For now.

While I slept, more tears in my fabric developed. A huge split now runs from just beneath my right breast, down my side, to the top of my thigh. A larger version of the woman once called Margot continues to outgrow her exoskeleton, like the little girl Alice after the 'drink me' potion. Soon I will slough this suffocating flesh off completely, and I do not know what I will be underneath, but that is part of the joy of giving birth to oneself, I suppose: the uncertainty of the new.

The smell of blood tickles the sensitive hairs lining my nostrils. I sneeze. I have little knowledge or prior memory of how I came to be here, in this state. What recollections I do have are jumbled, messy, a series of muted images out of sequence. I only know that something has happened. A threshold has been crossed from which I can never come back.

This feeling is compounded by a low, furious growl that fills the dark spaces around me. The growl is unlike anything I have ever heard before. My spinning mind cannot place it: not animal, not human, not mechanical. It sounds simulated, manipulated, a movie-night, hide-behind-a-cushion sound. It has no business being in this bedroom, where...

Bedroom. I am lying on a bed.

Also not mine. This place smells nothing like the house I share with Adam.

Adam.

His name, a punch to my heart.

This is the source of the wrongness pulling at my thoughts.

Adam.

My love.

But Adam is dead, a small voice reminds me.

It does not feel real to me. Not yet.

I sit up cautiously.

There is the tang of damp and rot in the air, and other uncomfortable things: soiled underwear, unflushed turds in a toilet somewhere close by, stale cigarette smoke, glue, vomit. Not home. Home used to smell of spices, of laundry detergent, of pencil shavings, of coconut shampoo. Of bleach and red wine and printer ink, of soy candles and coffee.

This place doesn't sound like my home, either. This place is all hard angles and unadorned walls and an uncarpeted floor. Drafts whistle through multiple gaps under doors, around window frames. The sodden bedding under me rustles too loudly, filthy, stained polyester grating against my soft skin.

I am sluggish, as if drunk, or...

Full.

There is a shape on the bed next to me. Stiff, cold. I put out a hand to feel it. My fingers meet sharp, splintered bone.

Not Adam.

Someone else.

Who?

My shoulders heave suddenly, a full-body earthquake. I shudder, I shake.

I can taste things I should not be able to taste.

A lump of something rises up from where I have pushed it down, climbing its way back up my gullet. Something gristly and bulky and solid. Breathing is suddenly difficult. I will choke unless I can evict the object.

Out, out!

I fumble for a bedside lamp, but there is none. It doesn't matter. My eyes adjust to the dark just as the obstruction shoots into my mouth, coming into focus at the precise moment I regurgitate the indigestible thing onto the soaking red bed.

It's a man's thumb, bitten off at the root.

The thumbnail, I can see, is dirty, ragged. He was a biter. Not fond of washing.

It's then that I remember: I am sharing the bed with a dead body.

And that body has quite a few missing parts to it.

Like this thumb.

Evidently, I feasted last night.

The growl, a low level threat until now, becomes a full-throated roar.

The roar lasts many, many years.

2.

My body, before I decided to live differently, always felt like an unruly garden in need of constant tending. Like Sisyphus pushing a boulder uphill, I fought a thousand tiny pointless battles with my own form, only to drop the rock and watch it roll back down again each time I looked in a mirror. I tweezed a hair; another sprouted back like a bramble. Rough dead skin was buffed and sloughed away only to build back up like algae on the surface of a pond. Moles were checked, wrinkles massaged, eye bags smoothed with compressions and cold flannels and special creams, all temporary fixes with no appreciable long-term benefit. My skin drank oils greedily yet never seemed to plump out. My hair was washed each morning, and by nightfall it had turned greasy, clinging flat against my skull, the ends knotted and split like dry straw. It was exhausting. Every day I found a new part of the garden that required attention. Stubble on my calves, eczema on my elbows, an ingrown hair on my armpit, an unsightly blackhead somewhere far too prominent to ignore, chapped and cracked lips, yellow coffee stains on my teeth, pubes matted and untidy. All the many, variegated parts of my garden were dealt with on rotation, and I felt trapped in a never-ending cycle of maintenance as I attempted to hold back the insidious fingers of age that spread like roots across my face and beyond.

I'm not even sure it was an attempt to hold back the years, when I think about it now. I began each new day poring over my reflection, fighting the usual revulsion I always experienced on seeing myself, fighting the desire to shed my skin and climb out of it and crawl into a new home, like a shell-less crab, a hermit crab picking a new suit of armour, creating a mental tasklist of things to fix, and I recall that, more than anything, it became habitual, this grooming. A nervous ritual I undertook because I felt I ought to. Or perhaps, because other people felt I ought to. I did not wish to seem complacent about my appearance. Complacency, I had been forcibly led to believe, was one step away from being slovenly. And slovenliness was not a desirable quality in a person. It might not have been a sin, but it was made clear to me from an early age that being clean was godly, as per the proverb, and I had been raised just Church of England enough to believe it. Beyond that, someone in my past, perhaps a relative, or a teacher, a friend, maybe even a movie or a book or an interview with a celebrity in a glossy magazine or a radio show, had created a sturdy link between presentability, and whether a person was good, or bad. It was coded into everything I consumed as a teenager. Saggy tits = bad. Bad skin = bad. Cellulite =

really, *really* bad, morally bankrupt in fact.

Smooth, shiny hair that bounced when you walked, however = good.

Angelic.

What a nice person you must be, with your neat cuticles and clear, acne-free face.

White teeth also meant you were superior, somehow. The rules didn't make much sense, but they were simple enough to follow. *Keep clean, people won't be mean.* I made that rhyme for myself when I was eleven.

As I hit puberty, my motivations evolved. It became more about survival. Other kids, I discovered, could be cruel, about anything, and were always looking for excuses to demonstrate this- especially the girls who grew breasts quicker than others. Once, during a lesson break, I stood with my back to a window reading a book, minding my own business. One of the girls in my class- a particularly mature fourteen year old called Amanada, who regularly wore designer perfume and immaculately applied eyeliner- began staring and pointing at my bare legs, which were illuminated by the beams of sunlight that streamed in behind me. Soon, a small crowd of teens were jeering at the backlit leg hair, crowing about how gross I was. *'Hairy Mary!'* they chanted until I left the room, and someone threw a half-empty can of cola at my head. It spattered over my shirt and neck, dried sticky, like shame.

I spent most of my lunch breaks from then on sitting under a tree at the far end of the playing fields, even when it rained. The nickname stuck long after I slunk home and furiously shaved every part of my body, including my arms and even my cheeks, until I was raw and covered in nasty, angry shaving pimples.

The hair grew back a few days later.

Not wishing to be singled out further, because life was complicated enough without the extra attention or aggression, I started the war with my body in earnest, and it consumed me. I waxed and epilated and conditioned and exfoliated and shaved and tweezed and bleached. I grabbed handfuls of soft flesh and squeezed them hard, wishing I could rip off the flab, sculpt myself like wet clay. I learned how to apply makeup, to artfully conceal blemishes, to make my eyes appear bigger, to highlight and exaggerate the curve of my lips. I studied the art of dressing 'for my shape', and wore only what was flattering. None of it ever made me feel beautiful, or like I belonged.

Rather, I often felt like I was rehearsing for a grand play that never opened. I looked the part, I knew all my lines, but the spotlight, despite everything I had been taught to expect, never fell on me. I suppose all people feel like that, when they are younger: big things are right around the corner. You are destined for more. You just have to believe in yourself, that's all. Wait, and rehearse. Your time will come.

And make sure your vagina is neat and tidy. The rest is a done deal.

3.

I asked Adam what he thought about this one evening when he was lying, face to groin, on my bed. Adam was particularly good at eating (trimmed) pussy, treating each opportunity to get down there as a special occasion rather than an obligation, taking his time with the experience, using his tongue to expertly explore and caress and tease the entirety of me rather than simply hammer the hard nub of my clitoris with flickering, single-minded puppy dog enthusiasm and hope for the best, so I was loathe to interrupt him, but I could not get the thought of my body, and how weary I was with it, out of my mind. I experienced a powerful flash of revulsion as I pictured how we must look from an outside perspective: his back, smooth and lightly muscled, freckles placed as if by an artist with a few expert, deliberate snaps of a sable brush, his thick hair curling tightly against his scalp, buttocks tensed like the marble sculptures you saw in art galleries, everything about him well put together, purposeful, beautifully proportioned...

And then, beneath him, the ragged patch of land that was me.

He was himself, completely. I was still pretending, even at my age.

'Would you mind if I stopped shaving down there?' I asked, without warning.

Slightly affronted that I was not on the brink of orgasm yet, Adam lifted his wet face from between my thighs and frowned.

'It would make *this* a bit more difficult, but…no?' he answered, although I was not convinced he was thinking about it as carefully as I would like.

'What about my legs?'

Adam shrugged, fingering my labia idly. 'I mean, I'm not mad keen on 'au naturel', from a friction point of view more than anything else, I suppose, but…egh. It's your body.' His head lowered back to my pleasure, his tongue sliding inside me with smooth confidence. I gasped, which made him chuckle, the noise muffled by my quivering thighs.

Distraction was fleeting.

'What if…I stopped washing my hair?' I squeezed this out through gritted teeth.

'What if you shut up and let me make you cum?' Adam mumbled crossly.

I laced my fingers through his hair and pushed his head harder into me, needing to move things along more quickly. My legs, freshly shaved and moisturised, draped over those wonderful shoulders, my feet crossed behind Adam's head. I had a gel manicure on my toes that was starting to grow out. I had an appointment for a redo next week, but was already thinking of cancelling it.

I shook my head, trying to fling the wandering thoughts away like water from fur, but nothing seemed to help. I couldn't connect my mind with my body, the two parts of me seemed miles away from each other. Perhaps they always had, but it was becoming particularly pronounced, this rift between all the parts of me. I started to feel a great despair building for no discernible reason, and tried valiantly to squash it down, thinking about Adam, and how hurt he would be if I didn't climax soon.

I decided to fake it, and began to rock into him, hips working a familiar rhythm we'd learned over time, and he slipped a finger into my arsehole as I cried out urgently.

'There we go,' he cooed, kissing my sticky thighs, moving up to my soft belly. 'Good lass.'

Afterwards, while he was washing his hands, I found I could not let the subject go.

'What if I stopped wearing makeup?'

Adam came back from the bathroom, hopped under the covers, and leant up on one elbow on his pillow, head resting in his hand. He was younger than me, only five years, but it showed. His eyelids had not started to droop like mine had on one side. He had fewer grey hairs too, and kept in good shape. I wondered what people thought when they saw us together.

'What do you want from me, Margot?' he asked, searching my face to try and get an understanding of what was going on in my head. 'I feel like you're trying to get me to admit to something.'

I bit my lip. 'I'm just curious. Would you still fuck me?'

He rolled his eyes. 'What is this? Of course I would.'

'That doesn't mean much, though. Men would fuck corpses if…'

Adam groaned and collapsed back off his elbow, head momentarily consumed by the pillow.

'I don't entirely like where this conversation is going, Margot,' he said, tiredly. 'We fuck because we love each other, because it works, because its easy and fun. Because you're my best friend and I happen to like, very much in fact, being inside you. You feel like home to me. Always have. Not because you shave and wear makeup or whatever.'

And yet I wondered how true this was.

'So if I stopped doing all those things…it wouldn't bother you?'

He gave me a beleaguered look, and I knew he was about to end the conversation.

'Nope,' he said, lying in the way that people do when they love someone, and don't want to hurt their feelings. 'And stop making generalisations about men. You're always telling me chicks aren't monolith. Works both ways, you know. Maybe I'll stop shaving, huh?'

I sighed. 'It's not the same, and you know it.'

'Isn't it?'

It wasn't, but I didn't have the energy to explain the many ways how.

4.

The next day, I skipped my morning shower. It didn't make a huge amount of difference to my hygiene or how I went about my day, one shower, although the change of routine set me off-kilter as I slipped into fresh underwear, scraping my hair back into a bun so I didn't have to feel how heavy and unruly it was when unwashed. I chose loose fitting clothes rather than the usual tight jeans, push-up bra and tailored jacket I wore, opting for a soft hoodie, slouchy bottoms and my gym shoes instead. My walk to the office was a great deal more comfortable than it usually was as a result. I began to resent the many times I'd hobbled in on heels, feet screaming at me the whole way.

'Jesus, Margot,' my colleague Natalie said as I slipped behind my desk, opposite hers. 'You okay?'

I scowled, logging into my emails. A hangnail stuck out from the side of my thumb. Ordinarily, I would open my desk drawer, where I kept a manicure kit, and nip the dead skin off so it couldn't aggravate me, but that day, I forced myself not to. I tapped the sharp protuberance with my index finger instead, and found I rather enjoyed how it felt against my skin. Like I had a little porcupine barb on my thumb.

'Margot! Seriously, you okay?'

I looked up at Natalie. She was scrutinising my outfit.

'What?'

'Nothing, just…you look a bit…dishevelled.'

I glared at her. 'Thanks. I just didn't feel like it today, was all,' I said, banging away on my keyboard.

'Feel like what?'

'Oh, you know.' I gestured loosely at the air. 'Hair, makeup, clothes, all that shit. Just tired of it, I guess.'

Natalie, who was easily suggestible, thought about this for a moment. 'Well, I did read somewhere that the natural look is in at the moment, anyway,' she eventually reasoned, not wanting to get into an argument with me. 'I saw this reel where, like, you reset your body by not washing your hair or wearing makeup, and…'

I let her prattle on, losing myself in the spreadsheets and emails that needed as much daily attention as my body had up until that point, but it was curious to watch how differently she behaved around me as the day progressed. Although it was subtle, her reactions to my instructions were notably less respectful than usual. Less deferential. As if my below-standards appearance levelled the playing field. She was my work shadow, two positions below me, and had always treated me accordingly, but by the time 5pm rolled around, that changed. She left the office with the list of things

I'd tasked her with only half-complete, waving a cocky 'Cheerio, then!' at me as she flounced off with an uncharacteristically jaunty bounce in her step. Usually she slouched away at the end of each day, moody and defeated.

On my own way out an hour later, I encountered my boss leaving a meeting at the same time.

'Hey, Margot,' he said, voice edged with concern. 'You're not sick, are you? You know you shouldn't be here if you are.'

I sighed. 'No, not sick, don't worry.'

'Oh.' A beat of silence. The tact-wheels, I saw, were frantically spinning. Eventually he settled on humour as the best approach.

'Laundry day at home?'

I laughed sheepishly. 'Something like that.'

'Well, hurry up and get sorted,' he said, smoothing back his hair. 'We have standards here, you know.' He winked at me and moved on, but I could tell my appearance bothered him. It wasn't a 'company fit', I could imagine him saying in the pub, later. This irked me, because the way I wore my hair or covered my face in powder or squeezed into an underwired bra had absolutely fuck all to do with how well I did my job, and we both knew that.

Standards, I was beginning to think, were a poor way of measuring worth.

I worried at the hangnail all the way home until it bled profusely.

5.

Adam was waiting for me with a bottle of Merlot, jiggling two steaks in a pan on the hob. He folded me into his usual welcome-back hug, sniffing the snape of my neck.

'Pooh,' he murmured, resting his chin on top of my head. 'Stinky baby.'

I was annoyed by this, but didn't say so.

'How was your day?'

He broke away and went back to ladling butter over the sizzling meat. 'Alright,' he said, 'Boring same old, same old. The client wants to add a skylight to the bathroom, so they can lie in the tub and stare at the stars. Saw it on Tiktok, I think. I spent an hour explaining how this was structurally inadvisable and they said they'd pay me an extra twenty grand to make it happen. You?'

I fiddled with my wine glass, examining the liquid's colour under the bright spotlights in our kitchen. 'Much as the same as yours, from the sound of it. Numbers and statistics and emails. Nothing I am doing is setting the world on fire, exactly. Oh, and don't cook mine too much, okay? I feel like rare meat today.'

Adam shrugged and flipped the steaks over. 'Well,

you know what I think. That job is beneath you, always has been. You should have started up your own company years ago, you'd be CEO by now. Filthy rich, I bet. I'd be a kept man.'

I squeezed his arse. I couldn't help myself when he was in the kitchen, hands occupied.

'I don't want to be CEO of my own company. I'd rather stay at home all day with you. And seriously, don't overcook that. I want it bleeding on my plate.'

He laughed, pulling my fillet from the pan with tongs and setting it to one side. 'No you wouldn't.'

'Wouldn't what?' I was finding it hard to focus now the smell of meat filled my nostrils. I found I was suddenly horny, too, which was unlike me after a day in the office. Usually I was too tired to contemplate anything more strenuous than pressing buttons on the tv remote.

'Want to stay at home with me all day. You'd be bored to tears after twenty four hours. You like working. You just need the right job, is all. Something that fires you up, suits your nature better. Not turnover and retention reports.'

He was right, but I didn't see an easy solution. I had been in my job for fifteen years, I was qualified, had trained extensively in company policy and regulation, and didn't have the money or energy to start from scratch, learn a whole new skillset, in a brand new industry. Not at my age. He knew this, but it didn't change his opinion.

'Never too late, Margot,' he was fond of saying. 'Age is just a number.'

But it was easy for him. Adam had known since he was a child what his passion was: building things. He'd started on that path young, with an apprenticeship, and was now a highly sought after architect. Award-winning, the sort celebrities hired. He largely worked out of his office at the bottom of our garden, a small cabin with a moss-covered roof (by design), an espresso machine and a small log burner, tastefully decorated with house plants, old train travel posters and brass fixtures and fittings. He had everything he needed there, and was highly content with his lot. Days would pass without him ever having to leave the house, which I envied him for. When he did leave, for a site visit or client meeting, I grew anxious, even if I wasn't at home myself. Adam was cement between the bricks: he belonged to our house. Him not being in it or near it was fundamentally wrong, like the sky being bright yellow and the sun being blue. I often worried that something would happen to the place while he was gone: a fire, a gas leak, the roof collapsing. I never had these thoughts when I knew Adam was home. He was akin to gravity: grounding, a force that bound everything together.

I took a bath after dinner, but only because Adam drew one for me and I felt guilty about refusing it. He'd laid out all my usual bath accessories: loofah, candles, salt scrub, shampoo, eye mask, face mask, hair mask, oils, razor, body brush, wine glass. I looked at it all sitting on the bath-buddy and thought: *what the fuck is all this, really? What is it adding to my life?* There was a magazine, too, folded open at a random page showing an advert for some sort of light therapy mask. The woman modelling it smiled inanely as red light blasted her skin from behind the mask. The smile was the only part of her you could really see under the ridiculous contraption. She resembled a robot from an eighties sci-fi flick. I didn't understand how a different colour of light was supposed to make someone look younger. There was a payment plan offered in small print at the bottom of the ad. The whole proposition made me quietly furious in a way I didn't wholly comprehend.

But the bath bubbles were piling high, and the water smelled of lavender and eucalyptus, steam curling enticingly up above the tub, and Adam had pulled up a stool so he could sit with me while I soaked. I found I didn't have the heart to decline the opportunity to talk with him at such close quarters, so I stripped off, feeling the general grime and weariness of the day sitting heavy on my skin, and slipped into the bath without protest, gasping as the scalding hot water dissolved all the aches and pains I didn't know I'd accumulated.

He washed my hair while I soaked, although I asked him not to. He was doing it to relax me, he said, but I suspected an ulterior motive: he didn't like me looking so unkempt. His fingers were both gentle and strong on my scalp. He rubbed and massaged and rinsed and squeezed my hair like he was doing laundry, and although I could not say it was particularly soothing, it did make me feel loved, cared for, in a way that never ceased to amaze me. I had never been tended to as a child. He seemed to have always understood this, had seen, right from the start, the girl who was not used to being held. Adam was unlike anyone else I ever met in so many respects: frighteningly perceptive, consistently calm, master of his own fate, happy with the path he was on, confident and quiet and patient and yet somehow, not pious or saintly with any of it. He existed in his own world, deliberately oblivious to how others chose to live in theirs, and he had a small, simple list of things he wanted out of life: for me to be happy, good sex, interesting projects to keep his brain occupied, a basic level of health and fitness, and a decent diet of red meat. Beyond that, he said, the rest was all nonsense. Like fancy wallpaper pasted on the walls of a castle. Superfluous to what lay beneath: solid, dependable stone.

I envied him for his worldview, always had. To me, life was complicated and frightening and tiring in so many ways. I knew I needed to stop living in such a fraught manner, I knew I needed to simplify my own hopes and dreams and fears, but didn't have the slightest clue as to how to go about it.

Which was why, I tried explaining to him, I was becoming so leery about my body and the upkeep it required.

'It's just so time-consuming,' I told him, snorting as he accidentally dumped suds in my eyes while rinsing my hair. 'All this maintenance. Think of all the other things I could be doing with my time.'

'Like what?' He asked, not in a scornful way, but as someone genuinely interested. 'What would you do if you had the time back?'

I felt a surge of resentment, not because this was an unreasonable question, but for the opposite reason: it *was* perfectly reasonable, and I just didn't have an answer.

'I dunno,' I replied, sulkily. 'Write a book. Take up painting. Go to the gym more.'

'But you don't like any of those things, Margot. You hate exercise, you haven't read a book in years, and the last time we went to an art gallery you called each painting 'indulgent toddler bilge'. '

'It's not that I don't *like* those things,' I rebutted with some indignation, 'I just don't like trying to enjoy them alongside everything else I have to do. It's too much. Spinning all these plates all the time. I could be a Pulitzer prize winning novelist if I didn't have to shave my legs every day, think about that.'

'I'm not sure Pulitzer prize winning novelists let a bit of leg hair get in the way of literary greatness,' Adam chuckled. 'There are many other moving parts to their success beyond grooming, or lack thereof.'

I could feel myself getting increasingly agitated.

'That's not the point. The point is…the point…'

I didn't know what the point was, and that was the most infuriating thing of all. My heart yearned for something, yearned to the point of physical pain, but I could not determine what, exactly, I was longing for.

After my bath, we made love, but infuriatingly, I found I couldn't fully put my mind to it even though I had initiated the act. All the while Adam was on top of me, moving in and out, the veins in his neck taught and tense as he worked, I was distracted by my own ugliness. By what I must look like from his perspective. Red and sweaty and rippled, like a week-old strawberry, my skin pitted, pores obvious for all to see. I knew if I brought this up Adam would glare at me like I had suddenly sprouted an extra head, but I couldn't help it. The further into me he sank, the more I felt my own lack. When he touched my breasts, I thought about how much they sagged. When he held my throat gently in one large hand, I was reminded of the folding skin gathering there. When he flipped me over and around and entered me from behind, I thought about my stomach flapping loose beneath me. I stared at my hands as they gripped onto the headboard, frantically searching for something to anchor me before I panicked and dissociated completely, and noticed I had two hangnails now. Another flap of skin had peeled away from the bed of my other thumbnail. I had a matching pair, it seemed. The symmetry was oddly pleasing, the only thing about my body I enjoyed. I picked at the new hangnail and found the motion soothing. The low-level, nagging sting of freshly peeling skin brought me back into myself. I felt immense relief as the hangnail turned into a ragged flap that got longer and deeper the more I worked at it.

Adam eventually turned me on my back again and came, eyes rolling back in his head and that singular, throaty *'ahhhhhhhh'* he always uttered at the crucial moment dropping from his loose, wet lips. He was so vulnerable in this state, so intent and focused, that I felt happy for him, but impatient, too, needing him to fall asleep so I could cover myself up and be truly alone with my thoughts.

Panting, he kissed me hard on the mouth (I flinched thinking about the pucker lines running around my lips), rolled off, and went to shower. While he was busy rinsing and scrubbing I knelt up on the bed, making sure the fresh ejaculate in my body ran downwards, scooping him out of me with a hooked index finger as far as I was able, and wiping his semen fastidiously onto a tissue, hoping against hope that I wasn't pregnant, so I wouldn't have to replicate my own, foul body in miniature, dooming another innocent person to the flesh prison I had grown for myself.

6.

The next day there was a big meeting with the board I had completely forgotten about, a meeting I knew I was lucky to be invited to, for it was intended to serve as an unofficial audition for promotion to a higher level role, if the hints my boss had been throwing at me in the weeks leading up to it were anything to go by. Distracted by what I was sure was the feel of something growing in my womb, although I knew that to be impossible, I had let the meeting slip my mind entirely. I arrived flustered and late, my reports out of order and unchecked.

I did my best, but found it impossible to concentrate as the thought of pregnancy swelled and took on formidable proportions like expanding foam in my brain, dominating every moment of the meeting. When lunchtime rolled around, I excused myself from the paid-for lunch, bolted from the meeting room, and rushed to the toilets to google 'morning after pill'. I found an online service that let me order the pill with relative anonymity, sending the prescription to a pharmacy a ten minute walk away, for collection within the hour. I paced the streets near my office with mounting anxiety as that hour ticked down, almost falling into the pharmacy five minutes before the hour was up. The pharmacist who served me was inscrutable, betraying no emotion at all as she bagged the pill up, but I imagined I could see judgement there anyway.

Back in the staff toilets, I swigged sparkling water from a scrunched-up bottle and swallowed the pill. My panicked heart raced as I felt it go down, and I had a wild moment of sheer hysteria as I imagined myself once again from an outside perspective, huddled in the cubicle, gobbling emergency birth control like candy, furtively stuffing the box and discreet brown paper bag it came in into the sanitary bin, jigging up and down on my toes to make the pill work faster.

What the fuck are you doing, Margot? Outside Me asked, incredulous.

I don't know, Cubicle Me answered. *Honestly, I don't.*

Adam would be so disappointed in me, I thought.

The meeting resumed after lunch. I sat miserably through it, feeling my insides yawn like a black hole. Any baby that survived the pill would be well and truly lost in the vast space of me, I thought, floating endlessly forever in darkness. I became increasingly sullen as the strangeness and implications of my own behaviour began to sink in, unwilling to contribute anything much of worth to the proceedings, nagging instead at the rough edges of my fingernails with my teeth until they started to bleed.

At one point my boss, annoyed with my recalcitrance, asked me pointedly if I had any comments on, or suggestions for, tackling the increased staff turnover rates.

I looked up, irritated at having my thoughts interrupted, and spat a crescent of freshly nibbled fingernail onto the table in front of the horrified executives, one of whom let out a weird, embarrassed laugh as they realised what I'd done.

I stared at the fingernail, and the few blobs of pink phlegm surrounding it. So did everyone else.

'I don't feel well,' I said, by way of explanation. Then I rose from my seat slowly. 'Excuse me.'

I left without a backward glance. I heard my boss apologise on my behalf, heard him try to smooth things over with more tame jokes at my expense, but none of it mattered, I realised. I thought I could feel the pill spreading chemical fingers throughout my insides. I felt both painful relief and tremendous sadness, and struggled to make sense of either feeling.

7.

At home, I told Adam about the meeting but not about the pill. He tried to run me another bath. This time I declined, and went for a long walk around the city instead. Adam watched me go, confused and a little perturbed. It was unlike me to want to be alone like this.

'Just be safe,' he said, eyebrows drawn into a worried line. 'Stick to well-lit areas.'

I rolled my eyes but promised I would.

On my walk, I met with a fox. It was skinny and brazen, fur matted, tail clubbed with filth. I almost walked right by it, but then a car passed as I neared a dark alleyway, and the fox's eyes blazed in the reflective glare, two round, burning spots in the gloom. I stopped so as not to scare the animal off. Eventually, the fox emerged from the alley and met me on the main road. We stood assessing each other, the fox's nostrils twitching, and I thought how beautiful it was. Poised, wary, but not frightened of me. We stood like that for some time, acclimatising to each other. I realised I had not met a single person beyond Adam who gave me as much joy as that crystalline moment with the stray fox, and I wondered if that was normal, to be in such a closed-off state, despite having done everything over the years to be presentable, to fit in. I had lots of acquaintances, but didn't have any true friends beyond my boyfriend, and I knew that this was perhaps unhealthy, but didn't know how to fix it.

I looked down at my chewed and jagged fingernails in the weak light of a failing street lamp and thought that the sharp fragments I had not yet ripped away from the nail beds resembled claws, in the right light. I noticed small hairs growing around the cuticles too, and frowned. Was that normal? It bothered me less than it should have.

The fox, considering me no threat, got bored watching me and sauntered off, shadow trotting along the road beneath it. I found I envied the creature's freedom, and wondered where it slept at night. Maybe if I saw it again, I would follow it, and it could teach me something about living.

8.

When I got back, well after dark, Adam was waiting in a state of mild agitation.

He let out a sigh of relief as I came in through the front door.

'I was worried about you,' he said, helping me off with my coat. 'Better?'

'Sort of,' I replied. 'I think I am going to quit my job.'

'Okay,' he replied.

I was expecting more of a reaction, but then remembered this was Adam, who was possessed of a fierce intuition I resented slightly, for it indicated he knew me better than I did.

He'd been expecting this declaration for some time, it seemed.

'Do you have a plan?' He asked, calmly.

'Not really,' I said, scratching at my scalp, which was starting to itch from grease. I could feel a small raw spot developing just behind my left ear. I picked at it. 'But you were right. Being there...its killing me slowly from the inside out. It's so fucking meaningless.'

Adam hugged me, and sounded proud as he

declared he would support me no matter what I decided to do next.

I thought then that I didn't deserve so much support, or trust, or dedication. I felt guilt churning in my guts for the pill I'd swallowed, even though Adam had never expressed any controlling behaviour over my body or the decisions I made with it, or even confessed to me any particular desire to be a father. He would be a good one, I realised. An amazing father in fact.

But would I be a good mother? I was less sure about that. My own mother had not been affectionate, or loving, or terribly interested in me as a child. She'd certainly never held motherhood up as something for me to aspire to. Rather, she had gone to great lengths to tell me how stressful, inconvenient, and terribly, terribly difficult parenting was. My ambivalence had grown over the years the more horror stories she told.

But her circumstances had been different to mine, I knew that. For one thing, she didn't have an Adam.

Bit late for all this self-examination now, isn't it? an inner voice taunted, but I wrenched that monologue off sharply, no leaky faucets tolerated here, thank you.

I felt suddenly very tired, and very much in need of sleep.

Adam climbed into bed with me and stroked my bare back with the tips of his fingers soothingly until I passed out. Once or twice, he used his fingernails to pluck a stray hair from me, hairs that had not grown where they now flourished previously, and I worried that my body was changing, but in a distant, dispassionate way, as if I was observing a dying tree from a distance. Leaves fell, one by one, drifting away, but that was alright, because in the spring, everything was reborn.

In my dreams, the fox walked beside me through an endless night, and we were both hungry, but the hunger was the uncomplicated kind, for food only, and when I woke the next day, I found I'd been crying in my sleep.

9.

I didn't get a chance to hand in my notice. My boss called me at nine sharp the next day and told me, in a fake-sad voice, that the company was undergoing a surprise restructure and that regrettably, my position was being absorbed into another and so they had no choice but to let me go. I listened to him apologise, and hung up without acknowledging his message or even saying goodbye. There was no point in pretending we had any sort of relationship beyond the workplace, so why bother with niceties? He'd have forgotten about me by the end of the week, and that was honestly fine.

Adam was angry on my behalf, but I felt only relief. It was one less thing I had to do: resign.

I was offered a small severance package, which I accepted via email. It felt like silence money, more than anything- the company didn't want me talking about how I was fired for biting my fingernails in a meeting. I knew I could have negotiated more, and Adam told me I should, that my company and now ex-boss were probably expecting me to push back, but I couldn't bring myself to care. Done was done. I walked away from the company with enough money, thanks to my long service, to see me through to the next job, and that was good enough for the moment.

What became glaringly obvious to me as soon as I was unemployed, however, was that I had no passions. No steer. No neglected wants or needs burning inside me that I could fulfil now I had a lot of free time. This realisation filled me with acute chagrin, for without the artifice of an office job, there was nothing. I sat at home feeling stupid and lazy while Adam made himself busy in his office, emerging only when hungry and sometimes not even then.

At first, I busied myself cleaning the house from top to bottom, then stopped when I ran out of things to move, dust, polish and vacuum.

Then, I sorted through my belongings and narrowed down my possessions, dabbled with yoga, batch-cooked mediocre vegetable chilli, bought some oils and made a mess on canvas, toyed with gardening, and started journaling, but the only missives I ever wrote down were single sentence declarations regurgitated from inspirational Instagram posts I'd scrolled through in the past that in no way reflected how I actually thought or felt about anything.

10.

Eventually, I went back to walking, mostly as a way of passing the time between waking up and bedtime. And discovered I had at least one skill: that of being able to place one foot in front of the other, over and over, until I was standing in a variety of different destinations.

Hours of city rambling followed, in all weathers. I found I liked early evening best because it didn't feel too dicey, safety wise, but was dusky enough to offer anonymity, and the traffic and road noises were less overwhelming. People lit their homes but kept their curtains open for a select hour of each day, and I liked looking in on how others lived. I saw walls painted every shade under the sun, I saw stacks of books, I saw art, I saw people playing musical instruments, I saw kids watching cartoons, I saw a woman stitching a giant tapestry. I saw cushions and couches of every perceivable shape and size and fabric. I saw a man hit another man hard across the face, forcing blood to spurt from his nose. I saw students having sex. I saw an elderly lady asleep in her chair, five cats balanced on her shoulders, lap and the back of her neck. Her false teeth were loose in her mouth. I saw dogs with their faces pressed up against glass, waiting for their owners to come home. I saw filth and I saw minimalism, I saw wealth and poverty, all jumbled up together as I plodded along street after street.

Walking in the evening also increased my chances of encountering the fox.

I didn't give it a name, for I didn't believe in that. I did start carrying around small ring-top tins of cat food in my pockets. After a few weeks, the two of us had regular dinner dates. I would flip over a recycling bin in the fox's favourite alley, open a tin of cat food, place it in the alley about ten feet away, and sit on the box, waiting. Eventually, the fox would come, nose first out of the shadows, little white-socked paws making no noise as she trotted over to the tin. I gathered, from the teats hanging low to the ground underneath, that the fox was female, and had young pups somewhere. This made her extra hungry and appreciative of my offerings.

A month after I was let go from my job, the fox and I were familiar enough that I started to follow her on her nightly wanderings. We walked together, padding along the dimly-lit streets in companionable silence, until we reached a part of the city I didn't know well, a small urban valley surrounded by terraced houses that crested the rise around it. The base of the valley, I later learned, sat on top of large flood tanks. As buildings couldn't be located there, the valley cradled a large patchwork of vegetable allotments instead, in varying degrees of abundance. The fox was fond of raiding the compost bins here for scraps of vegetable peelings and rotting fruit. I found myself perusing some of these scraps with her, in an act of solidarity at first, but then because I found I enjoyed the texture of fruit on the turn, soft and mushy and pliable. It was strange, how decomposing things suddenly no longer revolted me, but oddly liberating too. I watched the fox snacking on browned apples and found my own mouth watering, so I began to eat alongside her. Sometimes I had to pick writhing maggots out from between my teeth. After a while, I found it easier to swallow them down whole.

At night, when I slept fitfully in my super-king sized bed as Adam snored gently beside me on freshly laundered sheets, I fancied I could feel them wriggling in my stomach.

11.

Then Adam got sick, came down with the flu with little warning. One minute he was hale and healthy, taking calls and sketching things out on his big table in his cabin, the next he was lying on the couch, feet stuck out over the ends, shivering and blowing his nose and holding his aching head as if to stop his skull from flying apart.

It was unlike Adam to be so unwell; he prided himself on staying fit, well-fed and rested. His stubbornness did him no favours, in this instance: he insisted he was fine even as his temperature reached dangerous highs, as he sweated and shook and burned bright red in the face and went off his food.

But he never complained, not once, even though I could tell how dreadful he felt.

My daily walks went on hold. I decided to embrace the moment, treating our sudden quarantine like a miniature hibernation. I cooked hot stews and soups and made copious Toddies with lemon, whisky and honey. I filled hot water bottles, popped blister packs of pills, disposed of mounds of snotty tissue and blew up two giant air beds, laying them across the living room floor, covering them with fitted sheets, duvets, blankets and pillows and bundling Adam up in a soft cocoon on the new floor-bed. I then propped his shoulders comfortably against a large bean-bag and held a cold flannel to his burning forehead while we binge-watched all the tv shows I had lost interest in. When we got fed up with our concentrated diet of true crime documentaries and high-concept sci-fi, I turned the set off, put quiet music on, and let Adam doze while I prepared a bowl of boiled water infused with menthol crystals, so he could steam. When he got back into an easier, uncongested way of breathing I told him to lie back and spooned him, holding his entire body close to me as he fell asleep, and I thought about the fox as I drifted off too, curled up in her den with her cubs. I wondered if she missed me, if she was capable of that. I missed her, missed the way she trotted along just in front of me, bushy tail out like a rudder, occasionally looking back, her brown eyes always slightly wary, but intelligent, and sharp.

I thought I would hate my enforced indoors time, but found, to my surprise, that I needed to rest too. I had been going through so many changes, mentally and physically, and I realised I hadn't rested properly in a good, long while.

So I made the most of it. I lounged alongside Adam, and it was a peculiarly intimate experience, despite, or perhaps because of how awful he felt. We suddenly became the only two people in the world. We slept and cuddled our way through the week, and on the eighth day, Adam woke with a smile, eyes bright once again. He still looked tired, but his appetite had returned. He showered and made breakfast, singing softly to himself as he scrambled eggs in a large griddle pan.

'I lost weight. Want some?' he asked, but I shook my head, stretching out my back and my legs. My week with home-cooked food had crowded my guts. I was ready to forage again. I was ready to resume my dinner dates with the fox. I was glad Adam was better, glad my walks could resume. The streets and the allotment called to me, and by evening I was gone again. I left Adam sitting on the couch, the floor bed packed away, forlornly thumbing through the channels on our streaming service alone.

He continued to voice no complaints, for that was not his way.

12.

I resumed my rambling life with a vengeance, covering more and more miles as the days passed. I stopped bathing altogether. I no longer began my day scrutinising my own reflection, assessing my supposed flaws, rather, I avoided mirrors entirely, refusing to make eye contact with myself if I happened to pass one.

At first, ignoring my reflection as diligently as I would ignore a stranger I didn't trust felt rude, but I soon got used to the idea that I didn't *need* a reflected version of me. A reflection was simply light bouncing back from a flat piece of glass. Mirror physics had no bearing on how well my legs worked, or how hungry I was, or whether I had something stuck between my back teeth, or how deeply I slept at night, or the near orgasmic release of taking a large shit.

And gradually, as I learned to inhabit myself without a reversed doppelganger dogging every step, stabbing at my brain with the dagger of doubt, telling me to attend to this imperfection or that, I experienced a sensation that was completely alien to me, up until that point: one of a growing contentment, satisfaction even, with my form.

My arms, I realised, were strong, able to lift heavy things. My legs carried me for miles and miles. My eyes worked well in the dark, and my feet were reliable, swift, my hands and fingers dextrous, my grip firm. These were the things, I knew, that mattered. Understanding this made me deeply embarrassed for my former lack of gratitude. For the hours, days, weeks I had wasted.

I applied myself enthusiastically to the task of making up for lost time.

The more accepting I became, the more my physique responded. I let my nails grow out into natural, strong points. Before, they had flaked and broken before they could get to any considerable length. The tiny hairs around my cuticles got longer, more bristly, and a springy fuzz began sprouting through the skin below my knuckles. I thought my hands would be warmer, come winter.

My incisors grew long and sharpened into defined spikes that sometimes stabbed my lips if I ate too hastily. My back molars clubbed together and developed serrated edges that hurt my tongue until it grew a thick, grey protective crust. Toothpaste became a thing of the past. I got used to the perpetually sour taste in my mouth. I wore the same clothes day in, day out, while everything else I owned, all the designer dresses and jeans and shoes and shirts, lay folded in my wardrobe. Some of this was laziness, some of it because I resented the uniform of my prior existence, but most of my clothing choices came down to practicality: I needed loose fitting garments as my skin grew sensitive to the extreme. Strange rashes and raw patches developed overnight and then vanished, only to pop up elsewhere on my body, so I was never sure which parts of me would be sore or not. Sometimes, I found the skin on my elbows suddenly dry, and cracked, and those cracks would get deeper and run along my arms, only to heal a few days later until more cracks opened on my knees and ankles. Anywhere I had a joint, I found, was in a constant state of discomfort.

My trainers sported large holes where my thickened toenails pressed up against the fabric during my long walks. My roller deodorant went unused on the dressing table Adam had made for me out of walnut, which gathered dust.

My evening foraging habits grew more determined. I began raiding people's bins when they were left out the night before collection day, sharing any particularly good morsels with the fox, who was loyal to me now she had determined I was a good source of food. I marvelled at how well my digestive system coped with the half-rotten chicken carcases we nagged on, the rotten, mulchy tomatoes, the mould-speckled bread. Every day I expected to wake up and puke or shit out the things I'd eaten the night before, but every day, instead, I felt healthier, more energetic, more nourished.

And twice as hungry.

I found I began to crave meat above any other food type, but only dead meat. I liked it green and stinking. My new teeth made short work of discarded pork rib bones, poultry, beef trimmings, chitlins, lamb cutlets, chops and leg joints, burger patties, sausage links... I found a wooden pen behind a local butcher's shop that was poorly secured, and raided the meat bins there nightly, revelling in the overpowering stench that hit me in the face every time I lifted one of the bin lids. The CCTV camera monitoring the pen was broken, and nobody seemed bothered about fixing it, so I had an unlimited source of food.

Anything home cooked or freshly prepared subsequently disagreed with me, so I stopped eating during the day when I was in the house, and saved myself for my meat waste forays.

Meanwhile, my boyfriend kept his distance, watching me evolve as if observing me through a pair of binoculars: I was far away, an animal silhouetted against the sky. Every now and then he would try and tempt me with a bath, or encourage me to shower, and I would refuse politely, and then, as he got more worried and insistent, more aggressively.

Adam took up sleeping on the couch, and became quiet, withdrawn in my presence. He drank more red wine in the evenings when I was out rambling. A confrontation was coming soon, I knew, but he was allowing me time and space to work through whatever madness he thought I had to on my own, without intervention. I knew he would continue to do so as long as I needed, unless I was harming myself, which I wasn't. If anything, I began to feel happier than I had in a long while. The simplicity of my new existence scratched an itch that had long been out of reach in my brain: it felt like freedom, of sorts, although as time passed I craved green spaces instead of urban sprawl. I fantasised about trees and waterfalls and the ocean, pastures and mountains and flowers and a wild, raw wind. I thought about running along ridges, I imagined my bare feet splodging through mud. The city took on a prison-like quality. Traffic sounds hurt my sensitive ears. Brightly lit windows made my eyes water. Chimney stacks, television aerials, attic conversions and smog from thousands of exhaust pipes obnubilated my view of the sky.

I wondered what it would be like to live 'off-grid', as people said. In a cabin, or even in a cave, or a small hollow at the base of a tree. I wondered what it would be like to feel snow land on my skin, or rise with birdsong. I dreamed of sunsets bleeding into a vast, uninterrupted horizon, and whispering grasses, towering cloudscapes, fresh bones crunching between my teeth. Every day I woke, it felt as if I had become a little leaner, a little more toned, a little hairier. A soft peach fuzz built up on my cheeks, hiding the blemishes I'd been so disgusted by only months earlier. My hair, unwashed, greasy at first, and tangled, suddenly developed a thick, glossy sheen, like that of a well-groomed pelt.

Adam continued to observe me with caution,

constantly assessing the situation, worrying, fretting about how he could reach me, wondering how he could start a conversation that would lead to a good place: back to familiarity. We stopped having sex, even when I initiated it, because, he said, he didn't know where my head was. Was he scared of me? I couldn't tell. He certainly didn't want to admit one, inarguable truth out loud: my body now repulsed him, for it smelt unwashed, and of wild things, outdoor things. Faeces and dirt and sweat and food scraps.

I thought I would miss the intimacy, but the lack was harder on him than me. I had begun to think of mating as perfunctory, a means to an end.

Eventually, as I knew it would, the situation came to a head.

And after that, everything changed, and I wished, more than anything, that I'd loved Adam better.

13.

It was the anniversary of when we began dating. I had forgotten this, and did nothing to mark the occasion. Not even a card. Time had lost all meaning to me beyond sunrise and sunset. I had no idea of the date, or even the day of the week.

But Adam remembered. Six months prior, before my metamorphosis had begun, he'd booked a table in a local pub for us to go and celebrate. It was a fancy pub he had long wanted to take me to, with a waiting list a year long. Snagging the table when a last-minute cancellation came up was a small moment of victory for him, which surprised me, because usually, these sorts of things slipped beneath his attention radar: trendy restaurants, michelin stars.

He came to me with the booking notification on his phone screen, held it out for me to read, shrugged sadly.

'You probably won't want to go,' he said. 'The dress code is...'

He trailed off. His eyes, I saw, had big dark circles beneath them. He was not sleeping well on the couch.

His evident sadness put me in a dilemma. I knew this sort of thing was important to him. I knew he wanted to reconnect, to celebrate our time together. I was suddenly aware of the impact my behaviour was having on him. On us. Guilt crashed in like waves from all sides. I loved Adam, did not want to hurt him, but I knew I couldn't be seen in public the way I currently was without subjecting him to great ridicule, or worse, pity.

Which left me with a choice. Clean up (if I could, I had no idea if my body would even fit into any of the outfits languishing in my wardrobe anymore), make my boyfriend happy, betray my newfound identity and rising sense of peace, or…

Continue down my path, and leave him behind.

I took some time to think about it. Adam retreated to his cabin at the bottom of the garden while I gazed out of our bedroom window at the skyline, crowded with telegraph poles and satellite dishes, and worried at my nails.

Perhaps, I thought to myself, *I could tidy up just once,* for him, for this one, special occasion. To show him I still cared, even if my focus was on other things for a while. To give him a final glimpse of what would never return. I could do this, I *would* do this, I would bathe and shave and wash and style and paint myself, and we would have this last meal, this final supper, and then the old Margot could crawl off in the night, disappearing into the brambly shadows, and in her place something new would remain, and that creature, whatever she was, would be happy, at last, for life would be straightforward, her existence would be reduced down to the bare minimum, to the most basic of needs: eat, sleep, breathe. Dream.

For I still dreamed, only now, my dreams were full of hope.

I went directly to the shower, turned it on to the maximum temperature, grabbed Adam's razor (mine had rusted over), a hairbrush and a tube of scented body wash, and began the process of 'scrubbing up.'

It took a long time. The shower plughole blocked up with my hair. I sniffled as I shaved it off, for I felt odd and naked without my pelt.

I filed my claws down, scrubbed my tongue with an electric toothbrush, covered the growing network of splits in my skin with flesh-coloured sticking plaster, then covered my limbs with a long-sleeved, floor length dress. I crammed my feet into pointed, high-heeled boots and dragged a comb through my hair. The comb's teeth snapped off but I persisted, scraping the newly tamed strands back into a ponytail. I re-pierced my ears with large diamond drops, pushing through the skin that had grown over my original piercing holes, and finished the look with the bright, glossy red lipstick I knew Adam liked.

When I presented myself to him hours later, fighting the nausea that roiled in my stomach as the smell of soap and shampoo and moisturising lotion and toothpaste and his favourite perfume warred with each other for my attention, he looked up from his desk as if an angel had presented itself to him in an act of revelation. The shock, happiness and sheer relief on his face disappointed me in a way I never thought possible.

'Will I do?' I asked, feeling hollow.

He rose, came around his desk, engulfed me in a huge, crushing hug, and buried his face in my neck.

'Thankyou,' he whispered, and of course, he wanted to fuck right then and there on the floor. I let him, not knowing it would be the very last time. He orgasmed with an almost pained roar, and needed a shower himself before we made our way out for what would be, it turned out, the worst night of my life.

14.

The pub was crowded, hot and noisy, brightly lit by too many overhead lamps. Candles flickered on every table. Raucous laughter, cutlery scraping on plates, the mingled aromas of fifty different dinners being cooked and eaten...I knew I could congratulate myself if I got through the night without vomiting.

But Adam was joyous, and that, I thought, was worth the sacrifice. He came to life as the night unfolded, ordering the most expensive bottle of wine from the menu with uncharacteristic extravagance, insisting that we partake in the full three courses, holding my hand while he ate overcooked steak (I had asked for mine blue, and been disappointed), which made things awkward, but he seemed to need the affection so much, and I found myself once again in the grip of deep guilt for how lonely I had made him, even as a part of me argued that I had a right to live as I chose, to live freely, and happily, and that I could not always be responsible for someone else's state of mind, could I? Wasn't I allowed a little selfishness to explore, to grow, to become? It was all so confusing, and I spoke little as I tried to puzzle it all out in my head, but Adam carried the conversation just fine without me, rattling on with an almost manic effervescence I'd not seen before. He'd been bottling up so many things, I understood, things we would have spoken about on a day to day basis over dinner before I had started my nightly excursions. Now he had my attention again, he was making the most of it, his thoughts tumbling out like so many ball bearings spilling all over the table, and me, and I found I loved him fiercely, which confused me even more.

When dessert came, my boyfriend pulled a box from his blazer pocket, a box that fitted neatly into the palm of his hand.

As a rushing, roaring sensation built up in my ears, I saw him climb out of his chair, kneel down beside me, and flip the lid to reveal a sparkling diamond.

There were tears in his eyes as he asked me to be his wife.

I stared at him as if he were speaking backwards. I swallowed, over and over, words sticking in my throat. I hoped he would think I was overcome with emotion. I was; just not with any emotion he would have expected.

'I don't know where you've been these last few months,' he said, gazing up at me in earnest, 'But I feel hopeful that you're coming back. I can't wait to see what our future together holds. I love you, Margot. Please say yes.'

I nodded, held out my hand for the ring. Tears

streamed down my own face, but they were not tears of joy.

The entire pub erupted in cheers and applause as the diamond slipped onto my finger.

Two hours later, Adam was dead.

15.

We went for drinks after, to celebrate. Adam called his parents, who were ecstatic, and uploaded a picture of us, the ring extended out to catch the camera flash, to his university group chat. Congratulatory texts pinged in by the dozens. I texted no one. I hadn't used my phone for weeks now. When the battery had run low I had not bothered to recharge it.

One cocktail turned into two, then three, then four. I found I no longer enjoyed the taste of alcohol, or the things it did to my body, but it helped numb the incredible, acute sense of fear that now had me firmly in grip. I do not know what I was scared of, exactly, only that I was terribly frightened. My heart raced, so I drank another Old Fashioned. My palms sweated and itched, so I sank a shot of tequila. Once, I looked down at myself, and I swore I could see my fingernails growing visibly longer, sharper, turning back into claws, even as I watched them. Knowing this could not be the case, I drank another shot. And then one more. The noise and chatter in the bar swelled to an overwhelmingly loud wall of noise that physically hurt my ears, but I was able to lip read, instinctively understanding what Adam was saying even though I couldn't hear him anymore.

What he was saying was mostly nonsense about weddings and honeymoons and one day maybe getting a dog, starting a family. Adam had never been a good drunk, and his speech grew more slurred as the night crawled on. I started to feel oddly protective of him, for I had never seen him so unguarded, so soft, except for that anomalous week when he had been sick. The old version of me would have been thrilled at this.

The Margot sitting in the bar that night felt only trepidation. A premonition of things to come.

Instinct, I suppose I should have called it.

I should have paid it more attention.

16.

On the way out of the bar, it happened. Adam, drunk and giddy, misjudged a step and staggered heavily into a group of men passing outside, tripping the tallest, loudest of them up by accident.

The tripped man toppled forward as Adam's legs got tangled in his. He landed heavily on the pavement, cried out, swore violently, jumped back up to his feet, and spat at us.

His friends crowded around, jostling Adam as my fiance clumsily righted himself.

'Watch yourself, you fucking idiot!' the man screamed.

I felt as if the entire night had been building to this moment of crisis. My body began to respond, tensing in anticipation of violence. My teeth, now once again protruding from beneath my top lip, ached fiercely. I knew I did not have hackles, but they rose anyway. My skin prickled as the man, wired and furious, shoved Adam hard on the chest, forcing him back into a wall.

'You want to fucking start something?' he shouted. 'Come on, then!'

Adam, white-face and wide-eyed, shook his head,

raised his arms and hands up in a conciliatory gesture of surrender.

'It was an accident, mate,' he tried to explain. 'I just got pissed, tripped, sorry. I don't want to start anything, I swear.'

'I'm not your fucking mate,' the man, who was beyond reasoning with, snarled back.

I felt a snarl of my own start up in the base of my throat.

My hands itched fiercely.

I thought I could feel my calves stretching out.

I cricked my neck, took a step forward.

'You want some as well?' the man yelled, his eyes small, dark and filled with rat-like hate.

I found myself smiling.

No, not smiling.

Baring my teeth, top and bottom, and growling.

The man blinked, then laughed.

'You mad bitch,' he replied. 'Think that's funny?'

His friends, however, watched me with narrowed eyes, a certain unease in their body language as the growl in my throat rose in pitch and ferocity. It didn't sound, even to my wounded ears, like a human growl, or even a woman mimicking an animal.

It sounded wild, unnatural, and raw, and *hungry*.

The man was only further enraged as I took another step forward.

'Come on then,' he said, letting Adam go and facing me square on.

My growl became a loud roar, and I whipped out a

hand.

Claws slashed the man across his chest, shredding the thin fabric of his shirt.

Red blood leaked down a suddenly exposed chest.

Adam's eyes widened.

'What the fuck?'

The man's friends took another step back.

'Her fuckin' eyes, bro...there's something wrong with her fucking eyes, come on mate, leave it! It's not worth it!'

But the man didn't want to leave it. I had drawn blood. His own red mist had clouded his judgement. He was on something, I could tell. His pupils were huge, and there were little clouds of white saliva gathering in the corners of his mouth.

I slashed again. He dodged me, only just, ducking out of my reach, bending low, and gabbing an empty bottle standing on the pavement by the bar door.

He swung the bottle in a deadly, glinting arc, aiming for my head. I felt the rush of air, heard the object moving towards me at alarming speed. I knew his aim was true, knew I only had moments to move, but I never got the chance.

Because Adam, my Adam, who I never loved well enough, cried *'No!'*, and lurched into the path of the oncoming swing.

There was a meaty *thud!*

And a faint crunching sound only I could hear.

Adam's eyes rolled back in his head.

He folded silently to the pavement.

A large pool of blood spread out like a halo around

his skull, which had a large dent in it.

'Shit! You fuckin' killed him, Matt, you fuckin' killed him!'

The man, still holding the bottle, looked down at the body by his feet.

'I fucking did, didn't I?' he said, incredulous.

Then he smiled at me, turned tail and ran, following his friends who had already bolted. He chucked the bottle into the road as he went. It hit the windscreen of a passing taxi, rolled off the bonnet, and shattered on the road. The taxi driver swerved as his windscreen splintered, and rammed headfirst into a bollard.

None of this mattered.

Adam's eyes remained closed, even as I crumpled and gathered him in my arms.

I knew he was dead without feeling for his non-existent pulse.

I knew it as surely as I knew I had to kill the man who had run away.

Track him, chase him down, hound him, rip his throat out with my bared teeth.

But I could not bring myself to leave Adam, not even to give chase.

Instead I held him to me, and screamed, and screamed, and kept screaming even as the ambulance arrived, as the paramedics tried to pull me from his lifeless body. A circle of silent, scared onlookers gathered, but none of them were staring at the dead man I clung to. They were staring at me, eyes wide, hands covering mouths. A few began filming me on their phones until the police arrived and chased them away.

Even then I did not stop screaming. The noises coming out of me were not possible, they defied human physics, but I wouldn't, I couldn't stop, not until a man slid a needle into my arm, a needle filled with something cold that relaxed me instantly and sent me off into a void.

In the dark sleep that followed, I hunted.

17.

I went back to the place where it happened in the early hours of the next day, having woken in a hospital bed, alone, when the sedation wore off.

I was still dressed, although my boots had been removed. Hospital smells assaulted me from all sides: chemicals, medication, blood, other bodily fluids, and a thick, sour scent that I recognised as sickness, as injury, as death, concentrated and cloying.

I slid out of bed, glad for the solitude, glad for the lack of police or hospital staff. I did not want to talk to anyone, or give a statement, or commiserate, or be looked after in any way.

I only wanted one thing, and after that, I would disappear.

I padded through the ward corridors on bare feet, slipping out through double swing doors and down a stairwell, then out through the revolving entrance before anyone knew I had gone. I did not know if there was anyone to register my absence anyway: had my mother been told? Adam's parents? Did they know their son was dead?

I couldn't care about that now. I only wanted to go

back to where it happened, to answer the call of my rising blood, which surged around inside my body like angry breakers battering up against the sides of my heart, which had become as hard and obdurate as a cliff facing out into the ocean.

I walked across the city until I reached the bar and found a large puddle of Adam's dried blood still decorating the pavement. Crime scene tape marked out the area.

I could not believe this was it. I could not believe this is where his life had ended.

I dropped to my knees, sniffing the paving slabs. A man walking past stared at me. I ignored him, letting my nostrils flare, pushing my face as close to the ground as possible.

The smells covering the pavement were complex, a mesh of footfalls from human traffic and some animals too: dozens of dogs, another fox (not my fox), seagulls, pigeons, a cat. Not to mention piss, vomit, dirt, exhaust-fume grime, chewing gum, dropped food, bird shit, broken glass, flattened cigarette butts...

It took me some time to locate the scent I needed, but eventually, I caught it. Faint, yet followable. The man had been wearing a particularly nasty aftershave, and had smelt of booze and something else, something processed and best described as edged, like a cutting blade. The man smelled of damage, of sweat and adrenaline and thinly contained crazy.

Once I latched onto his signature, I found I could

smell nothing else.

So I followed the trail, eyes closed, ears pricked, and the city woke slowly around me, but soon I would be clear of it, clear of the noise and the mess and the muck and the glass and the metal and the concrete and the endless, ceaseless urban pandemonium. It would all be a part of my past. I would leave myself behind with the memories of all the years spent with Adam, with the ghosts of lovemaking and arguments and laughter and triumphs and disappointments and orgasms and tears and meals consumed and books read and places visited and battles won and all those moments in time would crystalise like drops of rain, I was sure of it, they would harden into a million glittering diamonds and fall to the earth and soak into the ground, and maybe, after a while, fresh green things would sprout where they landed, but first…

But first…

I began to run.

18.

I located my prey in a derelict house on the far side of a brand new, respectable looking but empty housing estate on the edge of the city, one that had been fenced off for safety reasons. There had been a fire in this property recently, judging by the blackened brickwork and brown upvc window frames. The gutted, unstable shell left behind seemed to be a hub of activity, despite the KEEP OUT, DANGER! signs stuck everywhere. Because the location of the house was right at the very end of a street lined with other houses yet to be sold, with only fields stretching wide beyond the street limits and a motorway flyover rising high on concrete stilts above that, the place afforded privacy, and had become a meeting point, I saw, for various activities, some legal, most not. People came and went by the hour, money was often exchanged. Motorbikes pulled up and zoomed off, teens on bikes too. Once, I even saw a police car roll up. The sole driver, a young male officer, climbed out, went into the house through the gap in the fence, and came out half an hour later, sliding something into his trouser pocket and looking furtively around him before getting back in his car and speeding off.

I took up position in a large hedgerow on an overgrown plot of land opposite and watched the house, waiting for a glimpse of the man who had killed Adam. My patience was eventually rewarded. He emerged from the house in the early evening, friends in tow, wearing different clothes and a smug, almost vacant smile on his face. He wore brand new sneakers, blindingly white, and I realised his other shoes were probably splattered with Adam's blood.

The men dragged out folding chairs, sat in a small circle drinking beer and smoking as night fell. I watched Adam's killer laugh and tell jokes and mess around, acting like a child who needed constant attention. When he wasn't grandstanding he was texting furiously on his phone, a big man with big plans, with contacts aplenty. He swaggered and gesticulated and generally held court, a sad king on a cheap, collapsable throne, his burned palace rising wearily behind.

I watched him, and waited, wanting him to be at his most unprepared when I finally came for him.

The men went back indoors as the darkness deepened and the stars popped out. A party started. Thumping music blared. Coloured lights beamed out of various fire-damaged window panes. Laughter filled the air. Bottles clinked and smashed. People trudged in via the field behind the estate, and then drifted off as nighttime turned to dawn.

At five in the morning, the music eventually stopped. I gave it another half an hour, to see if anyone else would leave. When all signs of activity ceased, I trotted over to the house, squeezed through the fence panels, and made my way indoors. My feet, no longer entirely flat, but arched high, tipped with dewclaws and freshly padded with furry sacs that spread my weight comfortably, trampled over cigarettes and plastic cups, discarded condoms, laughing gas canisters and greasy chip-wrappers. My toe-claws tapped the ground busily as I moved. I dragged my hands along the soot-stained hall walls as I passed between them, and the satisfying scrape of gouged plaster made me feel confident, at ease, almost. My breath leaked out fast and foul in front of me, and my teeth had grown so long they now brushed my chin.

I scouted the bottom floor of the house, which was largely empty apart from two girls asleep in each other's arms on a rotten couch that had been dragged into the scorched, water damaged living room.

Then, I climbed the stairs.

I found the man asleep in a mouldy bed that had been made up with old sheets and mildewed duvet. He was naked, limp cock held in his hand.

I smiled, flexed my hands. My bones suddenly felt too big for me, like they would erupt through my flesh at any given moment. Hair sprouted through skin that had grown thin as crepe paper, and I felt the beginnings of a tail tug at the bottom of my spine.

I rolled my heavy head around on my neck,

opened my muzzle, and roared. Thick slobber fell from my lips.

After that, I remembered little.

19.

I walk now, beneath the motorway underpass, through wasteland and scrub, skirting around the no man's land of industrial estates and the community waste tip, past docks and shipping yards, up onto a slipway, walking where only cars should go, but the road is unusually empty.

Then I am crossing a vast bridge over a channel. After that, I trudge through fields, following the path of tributaries and rivers, passing through herds of sheep and cows who rear back as soon as they catch a whiff of me.

I am taller than I used to be, and with every step forward I take, my body adapts, shifts, morphs. My bones, as I knew they would, protrude from my skin, erupting out at the knees and elbows, but that is okay, because there is new skin underneath, skin lined with thick, dark, impenetrable fur, and soon enough, I have sloughed off the old shape I used to wear, and it trails behind me like a ragged, torn flag until I leave it behind completely, lying stretched out in the mud of a freshly tilled field, a paper-thin woman with a name I can no longer remember, for names are useless anyway. The wind picks up, snatches the moult from the soil, whips it up into the air, and for a split second I see empty eye holes, I see the fragile, almost translucent shape of fingers waving, as if in farewell. Then the wind carries the thing away, but I have stopped watching anyway, my face forward into the day, my paws squelching and tearing up clods of earth as I run, just like in my dream, towards wilderness, towards quiet green spaces, towards waterfalls and fells and meadows and mountains. I know they lie waiting for me, and I know I can disappear into them, these high, remote parts of the world, and when I get there I will find a place at the hollow of a tree, and I will make a den for myself there, and I will curl up and fall asleep, and when the moon rises I shall rise with it, and I shall hunt again, and I shall feast on freedom, fat and round and delicious as a maggot on month-old meat.

12598450R00042